Cumbria Libraries

3 8003 04475 6823

KT-238-209

The
BIG-Hearted
Book

Nicholas Allan

Hodder
Children's
Books

A division of Hachette Children's Books

LIBRARY SERVICES
FOR SCHOOLS

38003044756823

Bertrams | 24/07/2013

£6.99

LSS

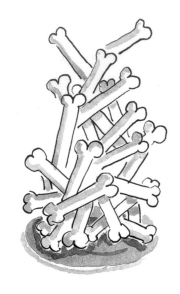

First published in 2013 by Hodder Children's Books

Text copyright © Nicholas Allan 2013
Illustrations copyright © Nicholas Allan 2013

Hodder Children's Books, 338 Euston Road, London, NW1 3BH
Hodder Children's Books Australia, Level 17/207 Kent Street,
Sydney, NSW 2000

The right of Nicholas Allan to be identified as the author and illustrator
of this Work has been asserted by him in accordance
with the Copyright, Designs and Patents Act 1988.

All rights reserved.

A catalogue record of this book is available from the British Library.

ISBN 978 1 444 91309 5

Printed in Italy

Hodder Children's Books is a division of Hachette Children's Books,
an Hachette UK Company

www.hachette.co.uk

Babette and Bill were joined
by a ribbon of hearts.
They were always together.

Through thick...

...and thin.

And when they were parted...

...they were broken-hearted!

They couldn't see the ribbon of hearts,
but it was always there.

Babette cooked for Bill –

even if it wasn't always her favourite.

Every day they went for a race in the park –

even though Bill ALWAYS won.

And at bedtime Babette ALWAYS had to read
Bill pirate and skeleton stories.

Until one day, Babette was too tired to cook.

And too tired to run.

"Come on!" said Bill. "Betcha can't beat me."
But Babette was too tired to care.

At bedtime she fell asleep before
she'd even finished the story!

Then, one morning, she was so very
tired she couldn't even get out of bed.

So Bill made a special lunch
– without a single bone in it.

But Babette still wouldn't eat it.

He tried to play a game Babette liked.

But Babette wouldn't play.

And when he read a princess story to her

Babette wouldn't listen. And then...

...she went away.

So Bill cooked and ran and read by himself.

At first it was fun.
But very soon he was off his food, off his running,
was sick of stories, and just lay in bed.

All this time Babette had been lying in bed too.

She had been ill, but now
her heart was on the mend.

It was getting stronger

and stronger and stronger.
In fact, so strong...

...it pulled Bill out of his bed

...and out of the door...

...and along the street

...and into the hospital

...and through the ward...

...until he found her.

Babette was better.

And when Bill went running with her in the park

he couldn't catch her!

Bill and Babette were together
again and this time...

...the ribbon of hearts
would never be broken.